IN THE STAR WORLD

A waterfall of stars fell into a beautiful pool. A snowy owl and a silver wolf stood beside it, watching intently as an image appeared in the water – a grey-haired lady holding a glittering black stone.

"I don't like this, Hunter," the wolf said. "She is full of bitterness and jealousy, and she is planning on harming the new Star Friends."

The owl nodded in concern and swept his wing across the surface of the water. The image of the old lady dissolved and reformed, this time showing four ten-year-old girls chatting in a bedroom. There were four animals with them – a fox, a wildcat, a young deer and a red squirrel. Each of the animals had unusual indigo eyes – they were animals from the Star World.

The wolf gazed at one of the girls – she had shoulder-length, dark blond hair and determined eyes. The fox was cuddled up to her side, resting his head on her shoulder. "Maia looks so much like her grandmother," the wolf said.

"I hope she has her grandmother's courage and cleverness," said the owl gravely. "These four girls and their Star Animals will have to be very brave if they are going to stop the one using dark magic. They will have to trust their instincts, their friendship – but, most of all, their hearts…"

CHAPTER ONE

Maia Greene sat cross-legged on her bed. Magic tingled through her, making her feel as if every centimetre of her skin was sparkling. Her Star Animal, Bracken the fox, sat beside her but her eyes were fixed on the small mirror in her hands. Through her bedroom door, she could hear her older sister Clio shouting to their mum that she couldn't find her favourite skirt.

"Show me where Clio's favourite skirt is," Maia whispered.

The surface of the mirror shimmered and a picture appeared. It showed a red skirt lying screwed up underneath the chest of drawers in Clio's bedroom.

"Found it!" Maia said in delight. When she had first started learning how to do magic, it would take her quite a while to connect with the magic current but now she could do it almost instantly.

Maia had been able to use magic ever since Bracken and some other animals from the Star World had appeared to find Star Friends. Only those who truly believed in magic could hear the Star Animals speaking. Together, a Star Friend and their Star Animal would use the magical current that flowed between the two worlds to help people. Each Star Friend had different magical abilities and when they used magic for good it strengthened the current.

Bracken nuzzled Maia, his soft fur tickling her skin. "You're getting so good at using magic!" he said.

Maia breathed in his familiar sweet scent – the smell of grass in the woods on a warm autumn day. "Good. I need to be strong if we want to stop whoever is using dark magic. We all need to be."

Maia's three best friends, Lottie, Sita and Ionie, were also Star Friends. Together they had discovered that someone nearby was using dark magic to conjure Shades and that this was weakening the magical current. Shades were evil spirits who brought misery and unhappiness into people's lives, and Star Friends could use their magic to send them back to the shadows.

"We'll find whoever is conjuring Shades and stop them," Bracken declared. "Are we meeting up with the others today?"

"Yes, we're going to Ionie's house later this morning. I thought I'd call in at Auntie Mabel's on the way."

Auntie Mabel had been friends with Maia's granny before she had died. She was the only adult Maia knew who could do magic – she wasn't a Star Friend like Maia but used crystals and stones.

Maia heard her sister shouting on the landing again. "Oops, I still haven't told Clio where her skirt is."

Bracken disappeared in a shimmer of starlight as Maia opened the bedroom door. None of Maia's family knew about him – the Star World had to be kept secret from people who didn't believe in magic.

Clio was standing at the top of the stairs shouting, "I've looked *everywhere*!"

"Wear something else then," her mum said.

"But I want to wear my skirt!"

Maia went into Clio's messy bedroom and hurried over to the chest of drawers. She crouched down. Just then, Clio came into the room. "What are you doing in here?" she asked.

"I thought I'd help you look for your skirt,"
said Maia. "Is this it?" She pulled the red skirt
out from under the chest of drawers.

"Yes!" Clio gasped. She frowned. "Did you
put it there?"

"No!" Maia protested. "Just a lucky guess."

Their mum appeared in the doorway. "Clio,
this room is a tip. It's no wonder you can't find
anything!"

"Mum! Maia's found my skirt!" Clio said.
"You keep doing this — finding things that are

lost. How do you do it?"

Maia hid her smile. If only Clio knew the truth! "I guess I'm just good at finding things."

"I think you're psychic," said Clio, staring at her. "You should start a YouTube channel!"

Maia laughed it off but thought perhaps she should be a bit more careful about how she used her magic from now on.

"Clio, I hardly think Maia's psychic," Mum said, smiling. "I think you're just very bad at looking. Now get changed quickly and I'll drop you off at your friend's house. What are you going to do this morning, Maia?" Mrs Greene asked as they both left Clio's room.

"I'm meeting the others at Ionie's house. Is it OK if I go to Auntie Mabel's on the way?"

"Of course," Mrs Greene said. "Auntie Mabel always loves to see you. Tell her I'll call in for a cup of tea soon."

"OK," Maia said and she hurried down the stairs.

CHAPTER TWO

As Maia cycled through the streets of
Westcombe, the coastal Devon village where
she lived, the frosty November air stung her
cheeks. Autumn had definitely turned to
winter now – the branches of the trees were
almost bare and there was a thin coating of
frost on the grassy verges.

As she cycled along, the locals she passed
smiled at her and said hello. It was hard to
believe that someone in the village wanted to
use magic to hurt people. But Maia and her

friends had dealt with a Mirror Shade who had been making Clio jealous of her best friend and a Wish Shade trapped inside a garden gnome who had made a little girl's wish come true in horrible ways. Then, last week, they had faced Fear Shades that were hidden in four little yellow stretchy men. The Fear Shades had made it seem as if people's worst fears were coming true. Luckily Maia and her friends had realized what was going on and had managed to send them back to the shadows, too.

We have to find out who is causing all this trouble, Maia thought.

Maia got off her bike and leaned it against the wall in front of Auntie Mabel's cottage. She glanced towards the cottage on the right, feeling guilty as she remembered how she and the others had suspected that the eccentric old lady who lived there – Mrs Crooks – was the person doing dark magic. The Wish Shade in the gnome had told them that the person who had conjured him was a woman and when they had first met Mrs Crooks they had suspected her straightaway. She liked to go out into the woods at night, she was very grumpy, she had lots of garden gnomes and Sorrel had even smelled Shades near her garden. But it had turned out that Mrs Crooks was just a harmless old lady who didn't like children very much and loved to collect garden ornaments and rescue injured animals in the woods.

Looking at the two gnomes sitting either side of Mrs Crooks' front door, Maia wondered who had put the Wish Shade in the gnome that had been given to Paige.

Auntie Mabel opened her front door and beamed. "Hello, Maia. I wasn't expecting you."

"I was on my way to Ionie's and I thought I'd call in," said Maia.

"How lovely! I've just made some of my chocolate cookies – the ones I know you like."

Maia took off her shoes in the hall and went through to the familiar lounge, with its displays of polished stones and crystals decorating the shelves. On the coffee table she spotted an open cardboard box filled with cute knitted Christmas decorations – there were penguins, snowmen and reindeer, all with beautiful sparkling eyes made out of tiny black crystals.

"These are lovely," Maia said to Auntie Mabel.

"Thank you, Maia. I've been making them to sell at the Winter Fayre this weekend. You are going to come, aren't you?"

The Winter Fayre was held every November in the village hall. There were homemade cakes for sale as well as Christmas decorations, cards and gifts. Maia's Granny Anne had organized it when she was alive and Maia had been to it every year for as long as she could remember.

"Yes, I'll be there," Maia said.

"It'll be strange without your granny this year," said Auntie Mabel. "But we'll make sure it's a really special one. The village shall have the fayre it deserves! Now come into the kitchen and have a cookie."

They went into the kitchen at the back of the house and sat down at the table. "Have you and your friends got any closer to solving the mystery of who is conjuring the Shades?" Auntie Mabel said as Maia helped herself to a cookie. "When I last saw you, you said you thought it might be Mrs Crooks. I've been keeping an eye on her and she does act suspiciously – going out into the woods at all times of the day and night and—"

"Oh, it's OK, Auntie Mabel," Maia put in.

"It's not Mrs Crooks. We still don't know who it is, though. But we think that whoever it is put stretchy men with Shades trapped inside them on to the packets of sparklers you gave us."

Auntie Mabel looked shocked. "Those little stretchy men had Shades in!"

Maia nodded and gave a shiver. "Yes. Fear Shades. They were horrible."

"But you've sent them back to the Shadows? How did you manage that?" said Auntie Mabel, intrigued.

"It was Ionie and Sita really," said Maia. "Ionie's a Spirit Speaker so she sent them back to the shadows and Sita discovered she has this amazing ability – she can use her magic to command people and spirits to do what she wants. If she orders you to do something, you have to do it."

"Really?" Auntie Mabel breathed. "That's a very rare ability. Your granny had it, too."

Maia nodded. She'd used her magic to look back into the past and had seen her granny using the same powers as Sita. Star Friends all had different magical abilities — Maia could use the magic current to see into the past and future and to see things that were happening elsewhere. Lottie could become very agile and fast, and Ionie could travel from place to place using shadows and command Shades to return to the shadows as well as casting illusions. At first they'd thought that Sita's magic just allowed her to heal and soothe. But then, last week, she had discovered she could command people and spirits, too. "I don't think Sita likes being so powerful."

"Well, if she wants to talk about it, she's always welcome here," said Auntie Mabel. "I might be able to help."

"Thanks, I'll tell her," Maia said. Suddenly she remembered something she'd been meaning to ask. "Where did you get those sparklers from, Auntie Mabel? The ones that the stretchy men were attached to?"

"From the garden centre," said Auntie Mabel. "Goodness me, if I'd known there were Shades in those stretchy men I never would have given them to you. I wonder who put them there? Have you tried using the Seeing Stone to find out?"

"No, but I have been using it to look at other things," said Maia. Auntie Mabel had given Maia a pale pink Seeing Stone to help her look into the past. Although Maia could use Star Magic to do that, she found it much easier with the Seeing Stone. "I've been looking into the past, to when you and Granny Anne were younger. I've seen you doing magic together."

"I'm glad you've been using it." Auntie Mabel smiled. "You're a natural with crystal magic as well as Star Magic."

Maia glowed proudly. "I'd better go," she said, checking the clock on the wall, "or the others will wonder where I am."

"Wait a moment." Auntie Mabel hurried through to the lounge and came back with four knitted decorations. "Here, give one to each of your friends to say how sorry I am about those stretchy men."

"Thank you," said Maia.

As she headed to the front door she noticed a large snow globe on the side table in the hall. She was surprised to see that it was empty apart from a thin layer of snow. "I've never seen a snow globe without anything inside before," she said.

"It won't be empty for long. This is going to be a very special snow globe," said Auntie Mabel.

"Why?" asked Maia curiously.

"Oh, you'll find out," Auntie Mabel said, tapping her nose. "I just need to test it first." Maia opened her mouth but Auntie Mabel said, "No, don't ask any questions. Like I said, you'll find out soon enough."

Maia put on her coat and helmet and cycled off as Auntie Mabel waved from the doorway. What had Auntie Mabel meant? *Maybe the snow globe is magic and she's going to put something special inside it as a present*, Maia thought excitedly.

Crossing the main road, she turned on to the lane that led down to the beach. Seeing Lottie and Sita arriving at the driveway of Ionie's house, Maia cycled quickly to catch up with her friends.

CHAPTER THREE

"Hi, Maia!" Lottie called, jumping off her bike. Her black curls stuck out from under her pink helmet. She pulled it off and readjusted the butterfly clip in her hair.

"Hello." Sita's gentle brown eyes sparkled as she whispered, "Are you ready to do magic?"

Maia grinned. "Always."

As Maia propped her bike against the fence she accidentally brushed her hand against some nettles. "Ow!" she exclaimed.

"Let me look," said Sita.

Maia held out her hand. Sita touched the nettle rash and concentrated for a second. The pain and tingling faded and the bumps disappeared.

"That's awesome," said Maia, inspecting her hand. "Thank you."

Sita sighed happily. "I love using magic to heal."

The door opened and Ionie looked out. "I thought I heard you. Come in!" They all hurried upstairs to Ionie's bedroom. As soon as the door was shut behind them, they called their Star Animals' names.

"Bracken!"

"Juniper!"

"Sorrel!"

"Willow!"

In a wave of starry light the four animals appeared. Bracken put his paws up on Maia's knees and licked her face. Juniper, a red squirrel with a bushy tail, jumped on to the dressing table and then from there on to Lottie's shoulder. He tickled Lottie's cheek with his little paws, making her giggle and squirm. Willow, a deer with a coat the colour of a conker, nuzzled Sita's hands, and Sorrel the wildcat wound through Ionie's legs purring happily, her tail high in the air.

When the greetings were over they all sat down on the rug, the animals happily cuddling up to their Star Friends.

"Has anyone used their magic since yesterday?" Maia asked.

"I have," said Lottie. "I was walking home from my piano lesson and I saw a cat about to run into the road. I used my magic to move really quickly, and I grabbed it and took it to safety."

"That's brilliant!" said Sita. "I used my magic to heal my baby brother after he bumped his head on the coffee table."

"Cool!" said Maia.

"Have you used your powers to command people yet?" Ionie asked Sita.

Sita shook her head.

"I'd use that power if I had it," said Ionie longingly.

"Why haven't you?" Lottie asked.

"I just haven't," Sita muttered.

Willow spoke up. "What have you used your magic for, Ionie?"

"Ionie's been wonderful," said Sorrel smugly. "Tell them, Ionie."

"I used my magic to shadow-travel to the park. We'd been playing there and my little cousin had left her cuddly monkey. I went to find it and bring it back," said Ionie.

"Very clever," Sorrel said approvingly.

Maia caught sight of Lottie rolling her eyes. Sorrel always acted as if Ionie was better than the rest of them. Maia didn't mind but it irritated Lottie.

"How about you, Maia?" said Sita.

"Well, I used my magic to find Clio's skirt this morning," Maia said.

"That's all you've done?" Sorrel said, not sounding impressed.

Bracken stiffened. "It might have been a small thing but it was still a good deed." He rubbed his head against Maia's leg.

Sorrel gave him a cool look. "Not like Ionie's."

"I bet Clio was pleased though," said Ionie quickly.

"Yes, the trouble is, now she thinks I'm some kind of weird psychic," said Maia.

"Mystic Maia," Lottie said, grinning. "You could use your powers to tell people's fortunes and earn lots of money."

Sorrel sniffed. "Do I need to remind you that magic should only be used for good?"

"Maia would be doing good – she'd be helping us!" said Lottie.

Juniper chattered as if he was laughing and Bracken yapped cheekily but Sorrel flicked her tail round her paws, a disapproving look on her face.

"Have you been practising looking into the past, Maia?" Sita asked.

"A bit," said Maia. She didn't want to admit she'd been using the Seeing Stone. Bracken thought she should only use Star Magic and she had a feeling the other Star Animals – particularly Sorrel – would agree with him. "Oh, I've just remembered something," she said, changing the subject. "I called in to see Auntie Mabel on the way here and she gave me Christmas decorations for you all." She took them from her pocket and handed them out, keeping a snowman for herself.

"Cute!" said Lottie, looking at her reindeer.

Sita looked at the penguin Maia had given her. "My gran would love this. She adores penguins. I'll give it to her."

"Wait!" Sorrel hissed suddenly, her fur standing up. "Those decorations could have Shades in." She pounced on the knitted snowman Ionie was holding and sniffed it suspiciously. "They're safe," she said grudgingly.

"Of course they are," said Maia as Ionie picked up the snowman and put it on her desk. "Auntie Mabel's decorations wouldn't be bad. She only uses magic for good."

"She did give you the stretchy men," Sorrel reminded them.

"But she hadn't even noticed them. She picked the packs up from the garden centre!" Maia protested.

Ionie looked thoughtful. "Maybe if we go there we might find out something about them."

"How do we get there though?" said Lottie. "I suppose we could ask one of our parents to take us…"

"I could shadow-travel us!" exclaimed

Ionie. Recently, she had found out that she could take other people with her when she was shadow-travelling. She jumped to her feet. "Come on!"

"Wait! What if your mum comes in and finds we've all gone?" said Sita.

"She'll be really worried," Willow added.

"I don't mind staying," offered Sita. "If your mum does pop in I can say the rest of you have gone outside or something."

"I'll stay, too," Maia said. She wanted a chance to talk to Sita about her new powers. "I will use my magic so Sita and I can watch what you're doing," she told Lottie and Ionie.

Ionie looked at Lottie. "OK, guess it's you and me then." She and Lottie had never been very good friends – they were both clever and very competitive – and they rarely did anything just the two of them.

"I guess it is," said Lottie, giving Maia a slightly panicked look.

Ionie walked to a patch of shadows in the corner of the room and held out her hand. Lottie joined her – and then they and their Star Animals disappeared.

CHAPTER FOUR

Maia and Sita stared at the empty shadows.

"I hope they're OK," said Sita anxiously. "What if someone notices them suddenly appearing in the garden centre?"

Maia pulled a small mirror out of her pocket – she always carried it with her in case she wanted to do magic. She said Lottie and Ionie's names and, in the mirror, she saw her friends stepping out of the shadows beside a display of lawnmowers. Luckily no one seemed to notice. "They've just got there. They seem OK. I'll check again in a moment." She lowered the mirror. "So how are you?"

"Me? All right." Sita shrugged, tucking a strand of hair behind her ear. "Why?"

"I just wondered how you were feeling about being able to command people," Maia said.

Willow nudged Sita encouragingly. "Talk to Maia. Tell her."

"Well, to be honest, I… I don't like it," Sita muttered. "I'm not even sure if it's real. I mean it could just have been a fluke when I stopped those stretchy men."

"It wasn't," Bracken said.

"No way," said Maia, shaking her head. "You told us to freeze and none of us could move until you freed us. Your power's real."

"But it can't be!" Sita said desperately. "I can't even decide what clothes to wear in the morning or how to do my hair. I *can't* be the powerful one."

"But you are," Bracken told her. "And that's good, isn't it?"

"No. It's a mistake," Sita said. Her eyes filled with tears.

"Look, don't stress about it," Maia said, squeezing Sita's hand. "Auntie Mabel suggested that you call in and see her if you want to talk. My granny had the same power as you and Auntie Mabel can help you." Not wanting to upset Sita any more, she changed the subject. "Should we check on the others again?"

This time when Maia picked up the mirror she saw Lottie and Ionie standing by a display of gnomes. "They're by some garden gnomes!" she exclaimed. "They look just like the one the Wish Shade was in. Maybe he came from that garden centre, just like the stretchy men!" Letting everything else fade away, she focused on the picture and heard Ionie speak.

"Let's ask about them," she was whispering to Lottie. "Then we'll see if we can find out more about the stretchy men later." She headed over to a nearby shop assistant.

"Excuse me, how much are the gnomes?" Ionie asked politely.

The lady smiled. "They're all different prices, the price tags are underneath them. They're sweet, aren't they?"

Ionie nodded. "Have they just arrived here or have you had them for a while?"

"They came in a few months ago now."

"I think my granny's friend might have bought one," said Lottie, joining Ionie. "It was a gnome with a four-leaf clover on his hat. Does that sound familiar?"

"Oh yes! He was very cute," said the assistant. "He had a message on the base. *Make a Wish*, I think it said."

Lottie nodded fast. "That's the one."

"Do you remember when he was sold?" Ionie asked eagerly.

The assistant nodded. "I do. It was about a month ago – and I remember the lady who bought him. She comes in quite a lot. She lives in Westcombe. Cheerful lady, quite small with grey hair and very blue eyes."

Maia's heart thumped. They had a description of the person who had bought the gnome!

"What's your granny's friend called?" the assistant asked

"Umm, she's…" Lottie gave Ionie a panicked look. "She's…"

"Oh, my phone!" said Ionie, pulling her phone out of her pocket. "It's my mum," she said to the assistant apologetically. "She's probably wondering where we are. Thanks for your help." She held up the phone to her ear. "Hi, Mum," she said, pretending to answer a call as she dragged Lottie away round the side of a display of toys. "Yes, we're just coming."

Lottie squeaked and pointed at a shelf where there was a big box of stretchy men.

"Stretchy men!" Ionie gasped. "I wonder if these ones have got Shades in, too. Sorrel, come here!" she whispered.

Maia caught her breath as she saw the wildcat appear. What if someone spotted her?

Ionie pushed a stretchy man towards the cat. "Has this got a Shade in it?"

Sorrel sniffed. "No."

"Ionie! Someone's coming. Quick!" Lottie hissed.

"Time to go!" said Ionie, throwing the stretchy man back in the box.

Sorrel vanished and Ionie grabbed Lottie's

hand and pulled her into a patch of shadows. They disappeared.

A second later they were back in Ionie's bedroom, giggling and stumbling out of the shadows beside Ionie's wardrobe. "Oh, my goodness! Shadow-travelling is fun!" said Lottie.

"It really is, isn't it?" Ionie gasped.

"What happened?" said Sita.

Lottie and Ionie called Juniper and Sorrel's names and the two animals appeared. Then they told the others what had happened.

"You both did exceptionally well," purred Sorrel.

Lottie grinned. "I didn't know what to say when the assistant asked me what my granny's friend was called. It was quick-thinking with the phone excuse, Ionie."

Ionie looked pleased. "Thanks. Your idea of pretending your granny's friend had bought a gnome was great, too. At least we know what the person who bought the gnome looks like now."

"She's got grey hair, blue eyes, she's quite small and she's from Westcombe," said Lottie.

They beamed at each other. Maia blinked. She didn't think she'd ever seen Lottie and Ionie act like they were proper friends before.

"There are quite a few old ladies in Westcombe like that," said Sita.

"I've got an idea," said Ionie suddenly. "All the old ladies are bound to go to the Winter Fayre this weekend. We can make a list of everyone there who matches that description. Then we can spy on them using Maia's magic and see if any of them act suspiciously."

"That's a great plan!" said Maia. "I think we've got some real clues to go on now." She held out her hand. "Go us!"

"Go us!" echoed Sita, Ionie and Lottie high-fiving each other.

CHAPTER FIVE

When Maia got home she hung her snowman decoration on the handle of her wardrobe door. As she called Bracken, she picked up the Seeing Stone from her desk. It glowed with a faint golden light. "I might try using the Seeing Stone to see Granny Anne and Auntie Mabel in the past," she told Bracken. She loved watching her granny when she was younger.

Bracken scratched his nose with a paw. "You're a Star Friend – you should use Star Magic, not Crystal Magic."

Maia reluctantly put the Seeing Stone into her pocket and sat down in front of the mirror on her desk. "Show me Granny Anne when she was just learning about being a Star Friend."

The surface of the mirror began to swirl. She waited for it to form a clear image but all she caught were brief pictures that appeared and then vanished – a young Granny Anne cuddling her silver wolf… Granny Anne with her hand on the wolf's back, smiling happily… Granny Anne arguing with someone… Maia squinted, trying to see who it was. It looked like it could be Auntie Mabel but before Maia could decide, the image flickered and was replaced by Granny Anne healing a horse's leg.

"What can you see?" Bracken asked.

"Just a whole load of different images flashing by," said Maia in frustration. "My magic's not working properly."

Bracken looked surprised. "It was working fine earlier. Try looking at something that's happening now."

Maia looked into the mirror again. "Show me … Auntie Mabel."

The surface swirled again and she caught a glimpse of Auntie Mabel holding the snow globe. She was smiling … but then the image swirled away.

"Auntie Mabel," Maia said again but nothing happened. "I can't even look into the present right now!" Maia gave Bracken a confused glance. "What's going on?"

Bracken looked puzzled. "It's very strange. Maybe you should have a break and try again later."

But that night Maia still couldn't see anything clearly. In the end, she gave up and fell asleep with Bracken in her arms.

✴ ✴ ✴

Maia woke up in a bad mood. It was a drizzly, grey morning and on the way to school Alfie

kept insisting on their mum stopping the buggy
so he could look at things.

"Cat!" he said. "Black cat."

"Yes, sweetie, that's right – it's a black cat,"
their mum said.

"Red car!" he said pointing to a shiny red
car parked by the pavement. "Wanna see!"

Mrs Greene pushed him over.

Maia felt irritation rise up inside her. "We're
going to be late, Mum!"

"No, we're not," her mum said. "He just
wants to have a look."

"He's had a look!" said Maia.

Her mum frowned. "What's up with you this morning?"

"Nothing," Maia muttered.

"Dog!" said Alfie next, pointing up ahead to where a brown and white spaniel was sniffing at some grass. The owner, Mrs Patel, who had been a friend of Granny Anne, was talking to Auntie Mabel.

Maia's mum went over to say hello.

"Hello, Maia. Hello, Alfie," said Auntie Mabel. "Off to school and playgroup?"

Maia forced herself to smile despite her bad mood. "Yep."

The dog licked Alfie's outstretched hand and stuck her nose in his face. Alfie giggled.

Maia crouched down to rub the dog's ears. Granny Anne had sometimes looked after Holly for the Patels when they went on holiday. "Hello, Holly dog," she said.

Holly bounced round Maia, her tail wagging really quickly.

"She's ready for her morning run in the woods," said Mrs Patel. "Any time you feel like dog-walking, Maia, do feel free to call by!"

"I will," Maia promised.

She spotted Lottie, Sita and Ionie walking together a bit further up the road. "I'll catch up with the others," she told her mum.

"All right, have a good day!" her mum called.

Maia hurried after her friends. Sita looked lost in her thoughts, her hands playing with the ends of her blue and white polka-dot scarf, while Lottie and Ionie were talking about the school maths club, complaining about how the games and worksheets were always too easy. Maia felt a flicker of jealousy as she saw Lottie and Ionie swap smiles and she tried to push the feeling away. It was silly to be jealous – after all, she had been wanting Lottie and Ionie to get on better for ages.

They all greeted her. "Are we going to meet

after school so we can talk about stuff?" Ionie said as they went into the playground.

"Yeah, and do *stuff*," said Lottie, raising her eyebrows meaningfully. They tried not to mention magic when there were other people around, in case anyone overheard.

"It's getting dark so early we probably won't be allowed to go to the clearing in the woods," Ionie said. "I'll ask if you can come to my house."

"That's a good idea," said Sita.

"I guess," said Maia a bit grumpily. She saw her friends give her surprised looks. "We went to Ionie's last time."

"We can go to yours if you want," said Ionie.

"No, it's OK," said Maia. She put down her bag and it fell over, spilling her books and lunch on to the wet ground.

"Stupid bag," she said crossly as the others helped her pick up her things and she shoved everything back in.

The bell rang and they
made their way over to line up in their
class groups. Lottie and Sita were together in
one Year Six class and Maia and Ionie were in
the other.

"Are you OK?" Ionie said, falling into step
with Maia. "You seem in a bad mood."

"I'm fine," snapped Maia.

Ionie stared at her. "There's no need to bite
my head off!"

As the day went on Maia's bad mood faded.
At the end of school, their parents agreed
that they could all go round to Ionie's house.
They were walking along the road when
Maia spotted a notice on a lamppost with a
photograph of a brown and white dog. She

frowned and hurried over. "Look! The Patels' dog has gone missing. I only saw her this morning!" She read the notice.

MISSING! PLEASE HELP!

Holly, our springer spaniel, ran off during her morning walk in the woods and hasn't been seen since. If anyone finds her or sees her, please contact us straightaway.

Call Kavita Patel – Westcombe 669324

"I wonder what's happened to her," Maia said.

"I hope she hasn't been run over," said Sita anxiously.

"Maybe we can help find her," said Ionie. "*With magic*," she mouthed, glancing back to where her dad was walking along talking to another dad.

They all nodded and hurried on down the road.

CHAPTER SIX

Ionie dumped her bag on her desk next to her snowman decoration. "I've got to find a place to put this," she said, holding it up.

"You could hang it from your mirror," suggested Lottie.

"I gave mine to my gran yesterday," said Sita. "She really liked it. She's going to buy some more at the Winter Fayre."

Ionie shut the door. "OK, let's call the animals and see if we can help find Holly."

The others nodded. As soon as the Star

Animals appeared and heard about the missing dog they agreed that the girls should try and find her using magic.

"Whose magic shall we use?" Lottie asked.

"Well, I think it's obvious," said Ionie. "We use Maia's magic to see where the dog is and then you and I will shadow-travel there. If it's trapped somewhere, you can use your agility to rescue it. Sorted!"

Maia bit her lip. Her bad mood felt like it was creeping back. Why did Ionie always think her plans were the best? "What about Sita?" she said. "That means she doesn't do anything."

"Maybe not everyone's magic is needed this time, Maia," Bracken said.

Annoyance flashed through Maia. "I think we should try and use everyone's magic."

"Why are you being so difficult?" Ionie said.

"Yeah, Maia, what's your problem?" Lottie asked, frowning.

Maia glared. They were all ganging up on her!

"I don't mind if I'm not needed," Sita said quickly. "If the dog is injured or needs calming down, I can help in that way." She squeezed Maia's hand. "Thanks for being a good friend though."

Maia felt the tension inside her slowly drain away. She started to sigh in relief but then she realized what Sita was doing. "You're using your magic on me!" she exclaimed indignantly.

"No! Well, not my commanding magic. It's only my soothing, healing magic," Sita said. "I was just trying to help – you seemed tense."

"I'm not tense!" Maia exclaimed. She

saw her friends and their animals exchange surprised looks and added, "Oh, this is stupid! You can all find Holly without me!"

"Maia!" Bracken raced up and put his paws on her knees. "This isn't like you. What's the matter?"

Maia took a deep breath and crouched down, burying her face in his fur. Breathing in his familiar scent, she felt her anger begin to fade. "Sorry," she said, looking up at the others. "I don't know why I'm in such a bad mood."

"Look, let's concentrate on trying to find Holly," said Sita. "Doing magic and helping people always makes us feel happy."

Bracken nuzzled Maia's cheek. "Can you use your mirror to try and find the dog?"

Maia nodded. She pulled the mirror out of her pocket and held it in front of her. "Holly, the Patels' dog," she told it, opening herself to the magical current. She felt it flow through her like a stream of glittering light, chasing away every

drop of irritation and tension. At first all she
saw in the mirror was whiteness
but then an image of the
brown and white spaniel
appeared. Where was
she?

Maia looked more
closely, searching for
clues. Everywhere
around Holly was just
white. Suddenly Maia
realized it was snow!

"What are you seeing?"
Bracken asked her.

"Snow," she said, feeling puzzled. "But that
can't be right." She glanced out of the window
and saw drizzle falling from the grey sky. There
was definitely no snow. She tried again. "Show
me where Holly, the Patels' dog, is." But the
image didn't change. "I don't know what to do.
My magic isn't showing me where she is."

"Don't worry," said Willow. "Me, Bracken, Juniper and Sorrel can go and look through the woods and countryside and see if we can find any trace of her."

Bracken jumped off Maia's knee. "We'll do it tonight."

"We'll find her," said Juniper. "And as soon as we do, we'll let you know."

Maia nodded unhappily, feeling envious of her three friends – their magic didn't seem to come and go like hers.

"You could use your magic to try and find out more about the person doing dark magic," Sita suggested.

Maia shook her head. "It never shows me anything if I ask it to show me that. Just blackness." Bracken had told her it was probably because the person was using dark magic to block herself from being discovered.

She got to her feet. "I think I might go home. I'm feeling a bit odd again."

"I'll ask my dad if he'll give you a lift," Ionie
said.

Maia followed Ionie down the stairs. The
happiness she had felt when she was doing
magic had vanished and now she just felt cross
and fed up again.

When Maia got back home, she put her school
things away and her eyes fell on the Seeing
Stone. She picked it up, wanting to forget the
day by looking into the past. She was about to
call Bracken's name when she hesitated.

*Maybe I won't bother him — he'll be busy trying
to find Holly*, she told herself. But she knew
deep down that it was an excuse, and that really
she didn't want him there because he would try
and stop her using the Seeing Stone.

Guilt flared inside her but she ignored it.
"Show me Granny Anne and Auntie Mabel,"
she whispered to the stone.

A picture appeared in the surface. Granny Anne and Auntie Mabel both looked about fourteen. Auntie Mabel had a crystal in her hands and was healing a scratch on Granny Anne's leg. Granny Anne hugged her and then Auntie Mabel showed her how she could use a different crystal to cast an illusion – making a rock beside the river appear to turn into a picnic hamper. Maia was impressed – Auntie Mabel could do so much with her Crystal Magic. Granny Anne clapped and smiled.

Maia continued to stare into the stone. She lost track of time as she watched image after image of Granny Anne and Auntie Mabel. She only stopped when she felt so tired that she couldn't go on any more.

She put down the Seeing Stone, feeling as if her energy had been sucked into it. Still, it had been worth it.

Maia placed the stone on her desk and called Bracken. He appeared instantly.

"Maia!" he said. "I've been worried about you. You didn't seem yourself earlier."

"I'm fine." Maia yawned.

Bracken sat back on his haunches. "What have you been doing?" he asked curiously.

"Just stuff." Maia shrugged.

"What stuff?" Bracken asked.

"Nothing important. Stop asking me questions!" Maia's words came out more sharply than she meant them to.

Bracken's ears flattened unhappily. Maia felt bad but couldn't bring herself to say sorry. She turned away and started tidying things on her desk. When she looked back, she saw Bracken had jumped on to her bed and was watching her. He looked worried.

The silence stretched between them, awkward and uncomfortable.

"I'm going downstairs to have tea," Maia muttered, hurrying out of the room.

By the next morning, Maia was still in a bad mood and it appeared to have spread to the rest of her family. Alfie was grouchy and Clio was banging around, trying to find her make-up bag. "Can't you find it for me?" she said to Maia.

"I can't find everything you lose," Maia snapped.

"Girls, please stop bickering!" Mrs Greene said as Alfie started to wail.

Maia grabbed her toast and stomped upstairs, leaving the chaos in the kitchen behind.

When she got to school, she saw Ionie waiting in the playground and went over to her. Ionie was holding a book on wild animals in Africa. Maia hadn't seen it before.

"Hi," Maia muttered.

"Hi," Ionie muttered back.

"What's the book for?" Maia said.

"For Lottie. Her class are doing their projects on endangered animals this week."

Maia felt a stab of jealousy. "Very friendly," she said sarcastically.

Ionie frowned. "Are you jealous?" she said. "You are, aren't you? You're jealous that Lottie and me are friends now!"

"Don't be stupid!" Maia retorted.

"I'm not the stupid one – you are!" Ionie shot back.

Just then, Lottie and Sita arrived. Lottie looked grumpy, too, but Sita was smiling as usual. "What's going on?" she said, looking at Maia and Ionie's cross faces.

"Ask *her*," Ionie and Maia muttered at the same time.

Sita looked from one friend to the other.

"Should I use my magic to help you feel better?"

"Oh yes, your incredibly amazing magic," said Lottie. "You're such a show-off, Sita!"

"I was just trying to help," said Sita, looking upset.

"Sita isn't a show-off!" Maia said angrily.

"You always take her side!" Lottie snapped.

"No, I don't!"

"Why are you all arguing today?" Sita exclaimed.

Their squabble was interrupted by the bell

ringing. The girls picked up their bags and
stomped away without saying anything more.

Maia felt like she had a black cloud hanging
over her all day. Lottie and Ionie seemed to
feel the same and no one suggested meeting
up after school. Maia went straight home and
shut herself in her room. She wanted to use the
Seeing Stone to see Granny Anne again even
though she knew Bracken wouldn't like it. She
thought about not calling him but she didn't
want to have to lie to him like she had the
night before. Reluctantly she called his name.

He appeared beside her. "How was school?"
he asked.

Maia shrugged. "Not great." She felt
suddenly cross with him. Why did he have to
make her feel guilty about using the Seeing
Stone? She picked it up from her desk. "I'm
going to use this to see Granny Anne."

"Maia, don't," Bracken pleaded.

"But it's better than the mirror," Maia argued. "I don't know why you're so funny about me using it." She stared into it and tried to ignore him. "Show me Granny Anne when she was younger."

She was soon engrossed in watching Auntie Mabel and Granny Anne doing magic together. When she finally finished, she turned round to find that Bracken had curled into a small ball on her bed. Maia longed to go and cuddle him but some part of herself stopped her.

It's not like using the Seeing Stone is really bad, she thought irritably. She got changed out of her school clothes without saying a word to Bracken, and then went downstairs. When she came back after tea he had gone and she didn't call his name until bedtime. Then he just curled up quietly by her feet instead of in her arms like he usually did. She turned out the light.

CHAPTER SEVEN

When Maia woke up the next morning, she found that Bracken had gone. She glanced at her bedside clock and realized it was much later than usual. Where was he? He usually woke her on school mornings with licks and cuddles.

"Bracken!" she called.

He appeared in her room, beside her bed.

"Where have you been?" she asked, getting up. "You didn't wake me and now I'm late for school." She looked at him.

"I... I was out looking for Holly," he said.

Maia felt guilty as she realized she'd forgotten all about the lost dog. "Oh, is that why your paws are muddy?" she said noticing Bracken's paws were flecked with soil. "Did you find her?" she asked as she started to pull on her school clothes.

"No, there's no trace of her down in the woods."

"I hope she's OK," Maia said anxiously. "Perhaps I should use the Seeing Stone to try and see her again."

"No, don't!" Bracken said quickly.

Maia frowned. The Seeing Stone wasn't on her desk where she'd left it. She crouched down to check the floor but just then her dad knocked on the door and opened it. Bracken vanished just in time.

"Come on, Maia. What are you doing? You're going to be late for school. You need to have some breakfast."

Maia had no choice but to follow her dad downstairs. *I'll find the Seeing Stone later*, she thought uneasily.

✦ ✦ ✦

However when Maia got back from school, she couldn't find the Seeing Stone anywhere. She called Bracken.

"It can't have just vanished into thin air," she said. "Have you seen it?"

Bracken scratched his ear with his back paw as he watched her search. "No."

Maia felt a flash of anger. "What am I going to do? I need it!"

"You don't need it," said Bracken, trotting over to her. "You can use Star Magic."

It doesn't work as well, Maia thought, but she didn't say anything to Bracken.

"You can," Bracken insisted, jumping up on to her lap. "Why don't you try now?"

"There's no point," Maia muttered, stroking

his fur. "It won't work."

Bracken cocked his head on one side. "Is that what you think?"

She nodded.

"But Maia, you mustn't think like that." He looked at her earnestly. "Remember when you first started learning to do magic, I said it would only happen if you believed it would. If you don't believe the magic will work, it won't."

Maia frowned. She'd forgotten that.

"Seeing magic *is* hard to control," Bracken went on. "But it won't help if you think it's not going to work."

"Maybe I'll try again," Maia said, feeling her bad mood start to fade. She stared into the mirror on the dressing table, stroking Bracken as she did so. "Show me, Holly," she said, hoping she would get more of an idea of where Holly was this time. She leaned forward eagerly as an image gradually formed in the mirror but it just showed Holly surrounded by lots of snow again. Maia couldn't understand what was going on.

She frowned. Was her magic working? She decided to try something else. "Show me Granny Anne when she and Auntie Mabel were my age," she said.

The surface of the mirror swirled like liquid silver and Maia's heart gave a leap as an image of Granny Anne and Auntie Mabel appeared. They were both wearing old-fashioned school uniform. Auntie Mabel was glaring at Granny Anne and speaking crossly. She could hear Auntie Mabel saying, "It's not fair! Everyone likes you, Anne. Everyone wants to be your friend. No one wants to be mine!"

"That's not true, Mabel," said Granny Anne. "I'm your friend."

"Yes, but you like everyone!" said Auntie Mabel, then she turned and ran away.

Maia sat back in surprise. She'd never seen Auntie Mabel and Granny Anne arguing before.

"Show me Granny Anne and Auntie Mabel when they start doing magic," she said curiously.

The image changed and she saw Granny Anne with her hand on her wolf's back, staring at Auntie Mabel who seemed to be hovering behind a blackberry bush as if she'd been hiding. "You mustn't tell anyone, Mabel," Granny Anne pleaded. "No one's supposed to know about Star Magic. Promise you won't say a word!"

Maia blinked. Weird. She'd seen this moment in the past before but it hadn't been like this. When she'd seen it in the Seeing Stone, Granny Anne had been excitedly telling Auntie Mabel that she had a secret to share with her. Now Granny Anne seemed to be begging Auntie

Mabel not to say anything – almost as if Granny Anne hadn't wanted Auntie Mabel to know…

"This is odd," Maia whispered to Bracken. "I'm seeing a different past to the one I've seen in the Seeing Stone."

"A different past?" He tilted his head. "But there can't be two pasts."

"I don't know which is real," said Maia. "Show me more," she said to the mirror.

The image changed and Maia saw Auntie Mabel in the clearing with Granny Anne. They were older now – teenagers. "I can do magic, too," Auntie Mabel was saying to Granny Anne, showing her a crystal. "It's not just you now. I'm special as well!"

"Yes," Granny Anne said slowly, "but you must be careful, Mabel. Magic should only be used for good. Please only do good things with it."

Auntie Mabel smiled slyly as she turned the crystal over in her hand. "We'll see."

Maia sat back and let the images fade. "In the

Seeing Stone, I see Granny Anne and Auntie Mabel as really good friends but when I look with Star Magic, it's not quite like that. Why?"

"I don't know," Bracken said anxiously. "But I think you should believe what the Star Magic is showing you."

Maia stroked him. "I wish I knew where the Seeing Stone was."

Bracken nuzzled her. "Maybe you should stop doing magic for tonight. We can talk to the other animals tomorrow and see if they have any idea about why the things you're seeing are different."

When Maia went to sleep, she had the first vivid dream she'd had in ages. Bracken had told her that her dreams might show real things now her magic was growing stronger. For a while they had – she'd seen the Fear Shades before they started affecting people – but for the last couple of weeks her dreams hadn't shown her anything at all. Tonight was different though.

In her dream, Granny Anne and Auntie

Mabel were in the clearing. They looked about sixteen years old.

Auntie Mabel's eyes were shining. "Crystals have energy inside them," she said to Granny Anne. "All you have to do is work out how to channel it and then you can use it for anything you want. You can make an object look like something else! They can heal, hurt, upset—"

"But magic should only be used for good," Granny Anne interrupted. "You know that."

"But why?" said Auntie Mabel. "We could get our own back on people who have made us miserable."

"No!" Granny Anne exclaimed. "You mustn't do that."

Auntie Mabel smiled. "When I possess the Dark Stone, no one will be able to stop me. Not even you." She laughed.

Maia sat up in bed, her heart pounding. Had her dream been real? It couldn't be. Auntie Mabel wouldn't use magic to do bad things.

Bracken was still snoozing beside her. Dawn was just breaking, the dark of night turning to a cold grey.

Maia went to her desk to look for the Seeing Stone. How could it have just vanished? Then she looked into the mirror and had an idea. Of course! She could use Star Magic to see where it was.

She opened herself to the magic current. "Show me where the Seeing Stone is."

A picture of her back garden appeared in the mirror.

But how can it be in the garden? she wondered.

"Show me how the Seeing Stone got there," she said curiously.

The image reformed. Ice seemed to run down her spine as she saw a fox trotting towards the flowerbed just as dawn was breaking. It was Bracken and he had the Seeing Stone in his mouth. She watched as he dropped it on to the soil, dug a hole and nudged it inside.

Bracken had taken the Seeing Stone. He had lied to her! Unless ... unless what she was seeing was false.

"Bracken!" she said, swinging round.

He woke instantly. "What is it?" he said, jumping to his feet.

"Did you take the Seeing Stone?" she demanded. "Did you bury it in the garden?" She was sure he was going to shake his head and tell her that what she had seen wasn't true.

But he looked down at the bed. "Yes," he admitted. "I'm sorry. But I didn't like you using it. There's something strange about it, Maia. I think it's showing you a false past and I think it's doing something to your Star Magic..."

"How dare you?" Maia hissed. She grabbed her dressing gown and slippers. "I'm going to get it back!"

"Maia!" Bracken protested. "Don't go!"

"You're the one who should go," Maia said. "I don't want you here!"

Bracken whimpered. "You don't mean that."

"I do! Go!"

Maia ran out of her room, down the stairs and through the back door. A light frost covered the grass and the air stung her cheeks. She ran to the flower bed she had seen in the mirror and spotted a patch of soil that looked like it had been recently disturbed. Crouching down, she used her hands to dig into the freezing soil. She caught a glimmer of pink and pushed the soil to one side. It was the Seeing Stone! She took it out with a sigh of relief.

When she came back into the house, her dad was in the kitchen getting Alfie a bottle of milk.

"Maia!" he exclaimed. "What on earth are you doing out in the garden at this hour?"

"I'd left something out there," Maia lied.

"Well, you don't go out at six in the morning! And look at the mess you're making on the carpet."

"Sorry," Maia said. "I'll clean it up."

"Just take off your slippers and get back upstairs," her dad snapped. "I don't want this to happen again."

Maia kicked off her slippers and ran upstairs. When she got back to her room it was empty. Bracken had gone.

CHAPTER EIGHT

Maia shut the door and walked slowly over to her bed. Her eyes filled with hot, stinging tears. Everything was wrong. Everyone was cross and arguing, and Bracken… She thought back to how she had told him to go and a sudden fear gripped her. He wouldn't have gone back to the Star World, would he? He *was* still her Star Animal?

She sat on the bed and put her face in her hands.

"Bracken," she whispered.

She held her breath. Nothing happened. Her heart felt like it was going to break into pieces.

"Bracken!" she whispered frantically.

She almost fainted with relief when a shimmer of starlight slowly appeared, a curling plume of light getting stronger until it turned into the shape of a fox.

Bracken stood across the room from her, his ears lowered sadly and his tail between his legs.

"Bracken!" Maia gasped, holding out her arms.

He crept slowly over to her, wagging the tip of his bushy tail and she gathered him into her arms.

"I thought you'd gone back to the Star World," she said, a tear spilling down her cheek. "I thought I wasn't ever going to see you again."

He licked the tear away. "You're my Star Friend, Maia. That means I'll be with you for your whole life. If you call me, I'll always come."

"I'm sorry." Maia hugged him as tightly as she could. As he snuggled in her arms, she felt the crossness that had been filling her mind drain away.

"I'm sorry I took the Seeing Stone and I'm sorry I lied to you," he told her. "I just don't like that stone. I think there's something strange about it."

"I won't use it again," said Maia. "And I… I'm sorry I snapped at you the other day. I've just felt so mixed up and confused. It's like there's a cloud in my head making me feel cross all the time at the moment." She frowned.

"Though it's not there now."

Bracken looked thoughtful. "I wonder if…"
He broke off. "Stay there. Let's try something."
He wriggled out of her arms and trotted across
her bedroom. "How do you feel now?"

Irritation started to flicker through Maia.
"Worse again."

Bracken bounded back and jumped into her
arms. "And now?" he said, nuzzling her neck.

The feelings faded.

"Better," said Maia. She frowned at him. "So
when I'm touching you I feel normal. Why?"

"The bad feelings must be caused by some
sort of dark magic," Bracken said, his indigo
eyes serious. "That's why they go when you're
touching me."

"Do you think there's a Shade in the
house?" said Maia, looking around her room.
"Everyone in my family has been in a bad
mood. Lottie and Ionie, too. Do you think
there are lots of Shades?"

"Maybe," said Bracken. "I think we need to speak to the others."

"I'll message them to meet me before school," said Maia. She jumped up to get her phone. As soon as she was no longer holding Bracken, she could feel the bad mood starting to take over her again but she tried to fight the feelings away. *I'm not cross*, she told herself firmly. *I'm not angry.* She sent a group message to the others.

> Must talk to you at school. It's important. Get there early. Mxx

A few seconds later, her phone pinged. It was a message from Lottie.

> I can't. Gotta go to dentist Lx

Maia wanted to talk to everyone together. She texted back:

> OK. Let's meet at break and talk then.

Her phone pinged once more. It was Ionie.

> What's going on? Ix

> Tell u later. But for now cuddle ur animals lots.

> WHAT?!!

Sita joined in.

> I don't understand. Sxxx

> Talk at schl. Try not to get angry. Mxx

And then, ignoring the flurry of question marks and confused emojis that started pinging on to her phone from her friends, she gathered Bracken into her arms and hugged him tight.

"So you're saying you think Shades have been making us argue?" Ionie said in a low voice as they sat on the wall at break time. They were all wrapped up in coats and scarves and hats against the cold.

Maia nodded. "We don't normally feel like this, do we? We don't usually fall out like we did yesterday. My family have been in bad moods, too."

"And mine," said Lottie. "Mum's been shouting loads."

Ionie nodded. "Mine, too."

"Mine haven't," said Sita, looking puzzled. "And I haven't felt cross. I have felt unhappy but that's just because everyone's been arguing."

Maia looked at Lottie and Ionie. "But you've felt like me? Like there's something making you feel angry with everyone."

They both nodded.

"I shouted at Sorrel yesterday," Ionie admitted.

"And I got cross with Juniper," said Lottie.

"I told Bracken to go away," said Maia.

"It's got to be because of Shades," Sita said. "Maybe they're just affecting me differently."

Lottie rolled her eyes. "Oh, because you're so special!" Her hand flew to her mouth. "Sorry!" she gasped. "I didn't mean that, Sita! I don't know why I said it. I feel all twisted up inside with horrible feelings. Maia's right. It's *got* to be because of Shades."

"But where are they? What are they trapped in this time?" said Ionie. "Why haven't Sorrel or Willow smelled them? They're both really good at sniffing out Shades."

"I don't know," said Maia. "Should we meet up after school and try and work it out?"

"I can't. I'm going round to my gran's," Sita said.

"And I've got piano until six," said Lottie.

"I could ask Sorrel to check my house really well," said Ionie. "And then later I'll shadow-travel to Maia and Lottie's and bring us all to yours, Sita. Can you make sure no one is in the den in your garden? We could meet there."

Sita nodded.

"OK, Maia and Lottie, be ready in your bedrooms at half six. Agreed?" said Ionie.

Maia felt a rush of irritation that Ionie was taking charge but she pushed it firmly away. "OK. And in the meantime, let's try really hard not to argue."

They all nodded. "Agreed."

Maia found it hard to concentrate at school that day. She realized she hadn't told the others about the different pasts she had seen when she was using the Seeing Stone and the Star Magic, but right now it felt more important to stop the Shades that were making them argue.

When she got home, she shut herself away in her bedroom with Bracken and lay on her bed cuddling him. A little later, she got a text from Sita.

How r u? Sxxx

OK. Did u see ur gran?

Yes. She wasn't in a v good mood either. Maybe there are Shades EVERYWHERE!

Maia bit her lip.

Want to talk? Mxx

After a few seconds her phone started to ring with a FaceTime call from Sita.

Maia answered it and Sita's face appeared on her screen. She looked upset.

"What if I'm right? What if there are Shades everywhere and they're affecting everyone?" she said.

"We'll get rid of them," Maia told her. "We're Star Friends. You'll be able to command them like you did with the stretchy men."

"If it works," said Sita. "I haven't tried it since… Maia, what if it doesn't?"

"It will," Maia told her. "But first we have to *find* the Shades. Did Willow notice any trace at your house?"

"Nothing," said Sita. "But maybe Sorrel has found something at Ionie's."

"I hope so," said Maia.

When it got close to six thirty they rang off and Maia waited for Ionie to appear. Even though she was expecting it, she still jumped when Ionie and Lottie stepped out of the shadows beside her wardrobe.

"Let's get to Sita's," Ionie said, holding out her hand.

Maia stepped into the shadows with Ionie and Lottie, and felt the strange sensation of the world spinning away around her. Then her feet touched solid ground and she realized she was standing in Sita's den. It was a garden shed that Sita and her sisters had put a rug and some beanbags in.

Sita had turned on a small table light, casting shadows against the shed walls. "We can't be long," she said anxiously. "Our parents might start wondering where we are."

"Did Sorrel find anything?" Maia asked Ionie.

"No, nothing," Ionie said. "She went through my whole house and she didn't smell a Shade anywhere."

"But there have to be Shades there!" said Maia.

"Maybe magic can disguise the smell," said Lottie.

"I asked Sorrel that," Ionie said. "She said nothing can hide the smell of Shades."

"It doesn't make sense," said Maia. "The bad moods have got to be caused by Shades because otherwise they wouldn't fade like they do when we're cuddling our animals."

Sita glanced out of the window anxiously. "I'm going to have to go in a minute."

"Let's meet up tomorrow morning," said Maia. "Is everyone free?"

They found out they were all free apart from Lottie, who had gymnastics. "I can meet you straight after," she said.

"Why don't we meet at mine at twelve," said Ionie. "We can go to the clearing in the woods. Maybe we'll think better when we're there because Sorrel says the current of magic is so strong."

"Then it's the Winter Fayre in the afternoon," said Maia.

Sita shivered. "It's creepy to think that the person doing dark magic might actually be there. We might speak to them without realizing."

"We've got to make a list of everyone we see

there who matches the description," said Lottie. "The sooner we find out who it is, the better!"

Ionie shadow-travelled them all home. After Maia had whispered goodbye and her friends had disappeared, she sat down at her desk feeling very confused. If there were Shades affecting them all, why couldn't Sorrel and Willow find any trace of them?

I don't get it, she thought, resting her chin on her hands and staring into the mirror. *I don't understand*.

Chapter Nine

Maia's dreams that night showed her a gloomy underground room with stone walls. She was trapped, unable to move and overwhelmed by the feeling that she had lost something precious. A woman in a hooded cloak stalked up to her with a dark crystal in her hand. Maia could not see her face.

"When I touch you with this, you will lose everything," hissed the woman. She lifted it towards Maia.

"No!" Maia screamed.

She woke with a start to find Bracken licking her face. "You were having a bad dream, Maia. You were calling out in your sleep."

Maia pulled Bracken into a hug, burying her face in his soft fur, and told him what she'd seen.

"What did the woman look like?" Bracken asked. "Was it anyone you recognized?"

"I couldn't see her face." Maia shuddered as she remembered the fear she'd felt.

Bracken cuddled her closer. "We have to work out what's going on. Maybe when you go to the fayre this afternoon, you'll find some clues about who the old lady is that's doing all this."

"I hope so," said Maia.

She lay in bed and stroked Bracken until it was time to get up.

She was just getting dressed when her phone pinged.

It was a message from Sita.

What r u doing this morning? Sxx

Nothing. What about u?

Nothing much either. I didn't sleep v well. Think I might go and see Auntie Mabel and have a talk with her about my power.

Good plan. Come here afterwards if u want.

OK! Sxx

Maia put her phone into her pocket and kissed Bracken. "I'm going to get some breakfast. Sita's coming round later. Maybe we can do some magic with her and Willow."

She went downstairs. Her mum was banging breakfast bowls on the table. "Are you OK?" Maia asked tentatively.

"No, not really. I've got so much to do," her mum said. "I need to help set up for the fayre this morning but I've also got to show someone round Granny Anne's house. And I said I would call in and help Auntie Mabel take some boxes of decorations to the hall."

"I can do that," said Maia. Then she could meet Sita there and they could both talk to Auntie Mabel. Maybe Auntie Mabel would be able to help her work out why she was seeing two different versions of the past.

"Well, I was going to drive the boxes of decorations to the hall," her mum said, "but I'm sure they're light enough for you to carry. That would really help." She smiled. "Thanks, sweetie."

"No problem. I'll go after breakfast," Maia said, putting some bread in the toaster.

✦ ✦ ✦

After breakfast Maia ran upstairs to tell Bracken what she was doing. "I'll be back as soon as I can," she said.

"All right." He licked her nose as she hugged him. "I'll see you later."

He jumped on to the bed and curled up into a ball, his nose tucked into his bushy tail.

Maia smiled. "I love you," she murmured, giving him a kiss. She picked up the Seeing Stone so she could ask Auntie Mabel about it and texted Sita as she headed out.

Are u at AM's yet? I'll c u there. Mxx

Maia cycled quickly to keep warm. By the time she reached Auntie Mabel's house, her cheeks were pink and she was slightly breathless.

"Good morning," said Auntie Mabel, opening the door when she knocked. "What are you doing here, Maia?"

"I've come to help you take the decorations to the hall – Mum's really busy with other things," said Maia.

"That's very kind of you," said Auntie Mabel.

"Is Sita here?" Maia asked.

Auntie Mabel looked surprised. "Sita? No. Why? Was she planning on visiting me?"

Maia nodded. "She's going to drop by this morning. She wants to talk to you about magic," she said as Auntie Mabel ushered her inside.

"Well, why don't I get you a hot chocolate while we're waiting for her?" said Auntie Mabel. "You go through to the lounge and I'll put the kettle on."

As Auntie Mabel hurried to the kitchen, Maia took off her coat and hung it in the hall, making a mental note that Auntie Mabel seemed as cheerful as normal. *No Shades affecting her*, she thought as she went into the lounge.

The boxes of knitted decorations sat on the coffee table. Maia picked one up and its black crystal eyes sparkled in the light. Although the decoration looked cute, the crystal reminded Maia of the dark crystal she had seen in her dream. She shivered and put down the decoration.

The large snow globe she had seen the last time she was here was standing on the mantelpiece. She went over to it and saw that it now had a little model of a brown and white dog inside, curled up, fast asleep. How had Auntie Mabel put that in there?

Magic? wondered Maia.

Then the dog yawned and sat up.

Maia squeaked in shock. The dog was moving! It shook itself and sniffed around in the snow. Maia stared. What amazing magic was making the model dog seem alive?

She skirted round it to examine the globe from a different angle. The little brown and white dog looked strangely familiar, Maia thought. It looked just like Holly, the Patels' missing dog! As she stepped to the side to get a closer look, she trod on something soft and glanced down to see a blue and white scarf with a polka-dot pattern. Maia froze. It was Sita's favourite scarf.

But Auntie Mabel had just told her that Sita hadn't called by.

Her fingers tightened on the soft fabric, unease quickening through her as she looked from the scarf to the snow globe. What was going on?

Then she heard a faint banging sound coming from the hall. Picking up the snow globe, she hurried to the lounge doorway.

Thump, thump, thump.

The noise was coming from the door under the stairs. Maia knew it led to Auntie Mabel's cellar. Her heart skipped a beat as she heard a faint voice. "Let me out! Please, let me out!"

"Sita?" Maia gasped in shock.

"Maia! Get me out of here!" Sita exclaimed.

Maia put the snow globe on the floor and started to pull back the stiff metal bolts on the door. "What are you doing in there?" she whispered as she tried to wriggle the top bolt back.

"Auntie Mabel locked me in," said Sita, her voice faint through the door. "Maia, we've got to get out of here. She's not good like we thought."

Maia felt like all the breath had left her body. "What?"

"She's trapped Holly in the snow globe! She's evil!" Sita said.

There was a laugh behind her. Maia spun round and saw Auntie Mabel standing in the kitchen doorway, watching her with an amused look in her eyes.

Chapter Ten

Auntie Mabel's smile widened as Maia stared at her.

"Maia!" Sita banged on the door, breaking Maia out of her shock. "What's happening?"

Throwing herself at the door again, Maia scrambled to pull back the bolts.

"Bracken!" she gasped. "Please come! I need you!"

He appeared in a shimmer of starlight just as Auntie Mabel pulled a dark crystal from her pocket and held it out towards the door, muttering a harsh-sounding word that Maia had never heard before. The metal bolts instantly turned red-hot.

Maia yelped and pulled her hands away, her fingers stinging.

"Let Sita out!" shouted Maia as Bracken bounded at Auntie Mabel, his teeth bared, and stopped in front of her, growling angrily. "Why have you locked her up?"

Auntie Mabel grabbed the snow globe from the floor where Maia had left it.

"Because I am going to stop you Star Friends from getting in my way," Auntie Mabel said. She held the snow globe in one hand and a large, glittering dark crystal in the other.

A shiver ran down Maia's spine as she recognized the crystal from her dream.

Bracken sprang forwards and for a moment Maia thought he was going to be able to snatch it — but then Auntie Mabel swung the snow globe at him. The instant it touched his fur, he vanished.

Maia stared at the empty space where he had been. "Bracken!" Her voice rose. "What have you done with him?"

Auntie Mabel held up the snow globe with a triumphant smile. Inside the globe, next to the little dog, there was now a small russet fox. "He's in here. And unless you do what I say, you won't ever see him again."

"Bracken," Maia whispered, horrified.

Bracken started to bark furiously – Maia could see his mouth opening and closing but she couldn't hear him. Auntie Mabel touched the Dark Stone to the bolts of the cellar door and they slid back of their own accord, opening the door.

There was a flash of brown and Willow came charging out, heading straight for Auntie Mabel.

"Willow! Be careful!" cried Sita.

Moving more swiftly than Maia would have thought possible, Auntie Mabel swept the globe towards Willow and, as it touched her back, the deer vanished.

"Two Star Animals are mine, just two to go!" crowed Auntie Mabel, holding up the globe. Inside Willow was standing next to Bracken, shaking her head and looking very surprised.

"Into the cellar with your friend!" Auntie Mabel commanded, looking at Maia.

"No." Maia shook her head. "I'm not going in there."

"If you don't, I shall smash the globe. And what will happen to your precious animals then?" Auntie Mabel's eyes met Maia's. "They'll be gone forever!" She held the globe up above the hard tiled floor.

"Stop it!" Sita cried, but Auntie Mabel ignored her.

Maia hesitated. What should she do? Auntie Mabel's hand started to swing the globe downwards.

"No! Wait!" Maia gasped. "I'll go in the cellar."

She joined Sita and, with a harsh laugh, Auntie Mabel swung the door shut, plunging them into darkness. As they heard the bolts being pushed across, Sita grabbed Maia's hands. "What are we going to do?"

"I… I don't know." Maia was struggling to take everything in. Bracken had gone and so had Willow… She and Sita were trapped… And Auntie Mabel had been the person using dark magic!

Maia peered through the gloom. They were at the top of a staircase that led down into the cellar. "Isn't there a light in here?"

"I haven't been able to find one," said Sita.

Maia drew on her magic. It tingled through her and her eyesight sharpened, letting her see through the gloom.

"There!" she said, spotting an old-fashioned metal light switch high up on the wall. Standing on tiptoes, she pressed it and a single bulb in the ceiling lit up. It cast a weak light. At the bottom of the wooden stairs, the shadows in the cellar seemed to make everything look menacing. Still, it was better to have some light than none at all.

"What's she going to do to Bracken and Willow?" said Sita.

"I don't know." Maia felt panic rising inside her but she forced it down. Panicking wouldn't help them – or their animals. "We have to get them out of that globe." She frowned. "How did you end up trapped here?"

Sita shivered. "When I came round to talk to Auntie Mabel, she said she would make me some hot chocolate. As I was drinking it, I noticed the snow globe. Did you see it? Holly's inside!"

"I know! I saw!" Maia said. "Then I noticed your scarf on the floor."

"I must have dropped it when I saw Holly," Sita went on. "I think Auntie Mabel put something in the hot chocolate. All I can remember is jumping up to leave but then feeling really dizzy. I must have passed out because when I woke up, I was in here. I called Willow and started banging on the door, and then I heard you on the other side. Now you're in here, too!" Her eyes filled with tears.

Maia hugged her. "Auntie Mabel can't keep us in here forever," she said. "When she comes back you'll have to use your commanding magic and make her let us out."

"It doesn't work," said Sita. "I tried when she was about to smash the globe but it didn't make any difference."

Maia's heart sank. "You were trying to use your magic then?"

Sita nodded. "I can't do it. I told you. It was just a fluke with the stretchy men." She wiped away her tears with the back of her hand. "I'm not that powerful."

"Don't worry," Maia said. "I'll come up with another way to get us out." She thought back over the last few months. So, Auntie Mabel had been the person doing evil all along. She must have attached the stretchy men to the packets of sparklers herself. Maia remembered what the sales assistant at the garden centre had said to Ionie and Lottie – an older lady with grey hair and blue eyes had bought the Wish Gnome. That must have been Auntie Mabel, too. And then there was the very first Shade they had faced – the one who had been trapped inside the old compact mirror talking to Clio. A picture flashed into Maia's mind of Auntie Mabel helping her mum sort out Granny Anne's cottage…

"Look what I just found in a drawer," she'd said, turning round to Maia with the compact mirror in her hand.

Maybe she took it with her and gave it to me on purpose, Maia realized. *She wanted* me *to be affected by the Shade – only I gave the compact to Clio. Auntie Mabel found the compact just after I had told her I had seen a fox with indigo eyes. She must have realized I was going to be a Star Friend.*

She felt sick. She had trusted Auntie Mabel. She had told her about Bracken and let her see the Star Animals. She had asked her for advice and taken it. When she had tried to do what Auntie Mabel said, her magic had stopped working as well. Why hadn't she realized?

Because I thought Auntie Mabel was Granny Anne's friend!

Maia remembered the two different pasts she had seen – one using Star Magic and one using the Seeing Stone. She pulled the pink Seeing Stone out of her pocket and it glittered in the dim light. No wonder Bracken hadn't liked it. It had been showing her lies about the past. She looked at the golden glow coming from it and groaned inwardly. She should have realized. Whenever something was under an illusion spell she saw a glow around it. "I don't believe you look like you do," she whispered.

The glow faded and the stone turned an ugly grey with a red eye-shape in the centre.

"What's that stone?" Sita said curiously.

"Auntie Mabel gave it to me," Maia said.

"She told me it would help me see into the past but it hasn't been showing me the real past. It's been showing me a past she wanted me to see. Auntie Mabel wanted me to think she and Granny Anne were really good friends. I guess she did it so that I would trust her."

"But they *were* friends, weren't they?" Sita said, looking confused. "Didn't your granny use to visit her lots?"

Maia nodded. She didn't understand that bit. Why *had* Granny Anne visited Auntie Mabel so often if Auntie Mabel was evil?

She threw the Seeing Stone away from her, down the stairs into the shadows, and heard it clatter on to the stone floor.

Just then there was the sound of the bolts pulling back. The girls jumped to their feet as the door opened and Auntie Mabel stood there, smiling at them, the snow globe in one hand, the Dark Stone in her other.

CHAPTER ELEVEN

"Let us go!" Sita said. She took a breath and Maia could tell she was trying to use her commanding magic. Her voice shook. "You must let us out of here."

Auntie Mabel laughed. "Oh no. You're not going anywhere."

She held up the glittering Dark Stone and Maia cried out as a stream of energy seemed to thump into her stomach. Arms windmilling, she fell backwards, and she and Sita tumbled down the stairs in a tangle of arms and legs.

They landed in a heap in the cellar. Auntie
Mabel chuckled and followed them down to
the bottom.

For a moment Maia was winded and
struggled to breathe. She rolled on to her knees,
drawing in gasps of air, and saw that Sita was
doing the same.

Maia was aware of Auntie Mabel moving
swiftly around them. But it was only as she got
her breath back that she realized Auntie Mabel
had drawn a circle around them using the
stone, leaving a glowing red line on the floor.

Auntie Mabel straightened up and murmured a word. Instantly an assortment of candles standing on ledges around the stone cellar lit up. They cast a flickering glow, letting Maia see they were in a large underground room with a table at one end covered in rocks and crystals.

"What are you doing?" Maia demanded, standing up and helping Sita to her feet.

"I'm using the Dark Stone to make sure you can't escape," said Auntie Mabel coldly. "I shall keep you here until your friends arrive. When I have their Star Animals, too, I shall use the Dark Stone to take away all your memories of magic. I will make you forget you ever knew about Star Animals and the Star World. When you stop believing in magic, you will no longer stand in my way."

"We'll never stop believing in magic," exclaimed Maia.

Auntie Mabel's eyes glittered. "You will not be able to resist the Dark Stone. It is one of

the most powerful crystals in the world. You're
going to have to say goodbye to your animals."

She held out the snow globe.
Bracken put up his paws
on the glass, looking
desperately at Maia. She
lunged forwards but
flames leaped up from
the glowing line on
the floor, licking at
her outstretched arms.
Maia sprang back.

"Why are you doing
this?" shouted Sita.

"Why?" Auntie Mabel
raised her eyebrows. "So that
I can be the most powerful. More
powerful than any Star Friend will ever be."

"I thought you and Granny Anne were
friends!" Maia said furiously, her eyes stinging
with tears. "I thought you did good magic!"

Auntie Mabel snorted. "That's what she would have liked. But then I found the Dark Stone and I knew that when I learned to use it, I would be able to do anything I wanted." Her voice grew bitter. "But before I could learn to use its powers properly, Anne managed to take it from me and use her commanding magic to stop me from taking it back. Every time she visited me she reinforced the command – and without the Dark Stone, I was powerless to fight back."

"So that's why she visited you so often," Maia said slowly.

Auntie Mabel gave a nod. "People thought we were friends but really she was just trying to get me to lead a normal life. A dull life without magic and power while she –" her eyes filled with jealousy – "she could carry on doing her magic. She had her Star Animal. I had nothing!"

"She stopped you because you were going

to use magic for bad things," said Maia. "You wanted to hurt people – just like you're doing now." She looked at the stone. "But how did you get the stone back?"

"Oh, I was so helpful when your granny died, wasn't I?" Auntie Mabel said with a sly smile. "I offered to sort through all her things and I found it. It was as if it was waiting for me." Her fingers clenched around it. "Now it's mine and I am going to use it to hurt all the people Anne wanted to protect."

"What do you mean?" said Sita.

"Those knitted decorations upstairs are so sweet, aren't they?" said Auntie Mabel. "I'm sure they'll sell out at the fayre today. Once they're in houses all around the village, they'll start to affect people, little by little."

"The decorations?" Maia said. "But they haven't got Shades in them. Sorrel checked."

"Oh, my dear, you have so much to learn. It's not only Shades that can cause trouble," said

Auntie Mabel. "Herbs, potions, crystals, spells –
they can all be used to release negative energy
that will hurt and harm. Like that Seeing Stone
I glamoured and gave to you. It showed you
a false past and it has also been sending out
negative energy to block your magic and stop
it from working."

Maia stared at her. Now she thought about
it, she realized it was true. Auntie Mabel
laughed at her stunned expression.

"You really have been so easy to deceive.
Those crystals I carefully sewed into the
eyes of the decorations will send out their
negative energy. People will start to fall out and
unhappiness will come. But no one will ever
suspect the innocent little decorations. No one
will be having a good Christmas in Westcombe
this year." She smiled in delight.

"We'll stop you!" Maia exclaimed.

"How?" said Auntie Mabel, raising her
eyebrows. "You're trapped here. Soon your

friends will be here with you, too, and then
I shall take all your memories of magic away.
If you don't believe, you can't make magic
happen."

"But how will you get the others to come
here?" said Sita.

"By using a little illusion combined with
modern technology." Her voice hardened.
"Star Friends always think they're so special.
But Crystal Magic is better. You each only have
a few powers – I can do many things!" She
walked to the table and put down the snow
globe. Then she held up the Dark Stone and
whispered Maia's name. The air seemed to
shiver and Auntie Mabel changed to look just
like Maia. "What do you think?"

"You won't fool Lottie and Ionie!" Maia
declared.

"You don't sound like Maia," said Sita.

Auntie Mabel held the stone to her throat
and muttered another word.

"I'll be back very soon," she said in Maia's voice and then, picking up the snow globe, she laughed and headed up the stairs.

Chapter Twelve

"What are we going to do?" Maia said desperately as they heard the cellar door shut.

"I don't know," said Sita. "But look, let me heal the burn on your arm first." She took Maia's arm and Maia felt as if a cooling breeze was sweeping over her skin, taking away the heat and pain. She watched the blisters disappear and the pinkness fade.

"Thank you," she said gratefully.

"At least I can still do that type of magic," said Sita with relief.

"I bet you can do your commanding magic, too," said Maia. Sita shook her head but Auntie Mabel's words were echoing in Maia's head: *If you don't believe, you can't make magic happen.* It reminded her of what Bracken had said. "Listen – when you try to do it, do you believe it will work?"

Sita hesitated. "Um … not really, I guess. It's not how I feel with healing magic. I know that will work."

"You need to believe your commanding magic will work, too," said Maia. "When the Seeing Stone was affecting me, I stopped thinking my Star Magic would show me the past. Even when I wasn't near the Seeing Stone, it didn't work. But once I believed it would, it did." Maia looked round for some way to escape. Right now, persuading Sita her magic would work wasn't the priority. "We need to get to Ionie and Lottie somehow and warn them."

Sita gasped. "My phone! We could use it to message them!" She pulled it out of her pocket and tried to turn it on but then her face fell. "It's not working. The battery must be dead."

"Or the magic in here is stopping it somehow," said Maia.

"Where's yours?" said Sita.

"In my coat in the hall," said Maia. "We've got to think of a plan. I wonder how much time we have. If Auntie Mabel is going to persuade Lottie and Ionie to come here, it'll take her a little while. I can use my magic to see where they are." She took the mirror out of her pocket and tried to relax. "Lottie," she whispered.

An image of Lottie appeared. She was just going into Ionie's house. "They're at Ionie's," Maia said to Sita. She watched Ionie and Lottie run upstairs and go into Ionie's bedroom.

"The others will be here soon," she heard Ionie say. "I wonder if we'll find out anything about the person doing dark magic at the fayre this afternoon."

Suddenly Ionie's phone rang and she picked it up from her desk. "Maia's FaceTiming me."

Maia frowned. Auntie Mabel must have taken her phone! "Don't answer it!" she pleaded, even though she knew they couldn't hear her.

"What's happening?" demanded Sita.

Maia shook her head – she needed to see what was happening. Ionie was answering the FaceTime call and a picture of Maia popped up on her screen. "Hi, it's me."

It was really odd for Maia to hear her own voice.

"Where are you?" Ionie asked, holding up the phone so Lottie could join in with the call.

"At Auntie Mabel's. I need you both to come here quickly."

"Why?' said Lottie.

"I've found something very important in the cellar. Come now."

"OK," said Ionie. "But what is it?"

"I'll tell you when you get here."

The phone went blank.

Maia's face paled and she told Sita what had just happened.

"We've got to think of some way to stop them," said Sita.

There was a crash and a clatter beside the table, and Ionie and Lottie appeared in the shadows with Sorrel and Juniper.

Maia's heart plummeted. It was too late.

Sorrel took one sniff of the air and her tail fluffed up in alarm.

"What's going on?" Ionie demanded, hurrying towards Maia and Sita.

Sorrel yowled and leaped in front of Ionie, tripping her over. Ionie sprawled on the stone floor. "What did you do that for?" she gasped.

"Dark magic!" Sorrel hissed, her indigo eyes flashing as she looked at the circle on the floor. She spun round, taking in everything in the room. "This place reeks of it!"

"Sorrel's right," Maia gabbled. "Whatever you do, don't try and cross over the circle drawn on the floor. Flames jump up at you. You'll get burnt."

Ionie scrambled to her feet and Lottie joined her. Juniper was next to her, looking around anxiously.

"What's going on?" Lottie demanded again.

Maia and Sita told them about Auntie Mabel. They both looked stunned.

"I knew it!" spat Sorrel. "When we were in her garden last, I smelled Shades."

"We thought it was because of Mrs Crooks," said Maia, "but it must have been because of Auntie Mabel. She has a stone that's really powerful. Granny Anne took it from her a long time ago and then visited her every day to keep commanding her not to use dark magic. But when Granny Anne died, Auntie Mabel got the stone back."

"I just can't believe it," said Lottie, shaking her head.

"It's true," said Sita. She told them about the illusion Auntie Mabel had cast to make herself look and sound like Maia. "She's probably waiting for you at the front door right now."

"Why did you come to the cellar?" said Maia.

"Well, you said you'd found something important here – I wanted to find out what it was," said Ionie.

"Ionie's so brave," said Sorrel, purring approvingly and weaving between Ionie's legs.

"I tried to stop her," said Lottie. "Though I'm kind of glad she didn't listen to me now. At least we didn't walk straight into a trap."

"Where are Bracken and Willow?" said Juniper looking around.

Maia's heart twisted. "They're stuck inside a snow globe and Holly, the Patels' dog, is with them!" she explained. "It must be why I kept seeing Holly in snow. Auntie Mabel told me she was going to test the globe. I think she tried out the magic on Holly – maybe because Mrs Patel was one of Granny Anne's friends and she wanted to hurt her, just like she's been trying to hurt me and my family. Now Bracken and Willow are trapped inside it, too."

Juniper chattered unhappily and Sorrel bristled. "This is very bad news," she said. "If the old woman has them in her power, you'll have to do as she says."

"We've got to be able to stop her somehow," said Ionie desperately.

At that moment the cellar door opened.

"Hide!" Maia mouthed quickly.

Lottie hid behind the table while Ionie ran
to the wall and cast a glamour. She immediately
seemed to merge with the wall. Juniper and
Sorrel disappeared.

"Your friends will be here very soon," said
Auntie Mabel, coming down the stairs with
the snow globe. She looked her usual self again.
"But I don't think we need wait for them
to begin. It's time to start taking away your
memories of magic." She touched the Dark
Stone to the floor and the circle around Maia
and Sita vanished. "Who is going to be first?"
she said with an evil smile.

A Shade stepped out from the shadows by
the wall. It was tall and thin with spiny fingers
and sharp teeth. "How about me?" it hissed,
flexing its fingers.

Chapter Thirteen

Auntie Mabel exclaimed in shock. Maia froze
but then noticed the Shade had a glowing
golden outline and realized it was Ionie using
her magic to cast an illusion.

"What are you doing here? Who conjured
you from the shadows?" Auntie Mabel backed
away and stumbled on the Seeing Stone that
Maia had thrown into the cellar earlier. Losing
her balance, she fell to the ground.

There was a sudden blur of movement – it
was Lottie darting out from behind the table.

She grabbed the snow globe from Auntie Mabel's hands before the old lady realized what was happening.

"No!" shrieked Auntie Mabel, scrabbling after her on her hands and knees. But Lottie was already safely on the other side of the room, cradling the snow globe in her hands.

The Shade became Ionie once more. "Smash the globe, Lottie!"

"If you do, the animals will disappear forever!" hissed Auntie Mabel.

Ionie hesitated but then shook her head. "No, I don't believe you. When we smashed the mirror it *released* the Mirror Shade."

"Yes, and when the garden gnome smashed, it set the Wish Shade inside it free," said Lottie.

"You're right!" urged Juniper, leaping on to the table with the crystals. "Do it, Lottie!"

Auntie Mabel held up the Dark Stone and opened her mouth.

Maia's heart leaped into her throat. She was sure Auntie Mabel was going to use some sort of horrible power on Lottie. She couldn't let that happen. Throwing herself at Auntie Mabel, she grabbed the stone and wrestled it out of her fingers. "Got it!" she gasped in triumph.

Auntie Mabel's eyes glittered. "And so you have!" she spat. She pointed at Maia from the floor and screamed out a string of harsh-sounding words that Maia couldn't understand.

Maia felt the world spin and then it seemed as though her head was getting lighter and lighter. Her thoughts grew fuzzy and confused, and all she could hear were the strange-sounding words. She sank down to her knees, still holding the Dark Stone in her hands.

"What's happening?" Maia heard Ionie cry. "What's she doing to Maia?"

"Stop it!" Sita shouted, pointing at Auntie Mabel. Her voice was suddenly strong and clear. "I command you to be silent!"

Auntie Mabel's mouth opened and closed but no sound came out. With a yowl, Sorrel pounced on the old lady's chest and Lottie threw the globe on to the floor. There was a huge smash and it exploded into smithereens.

The next instant Bracken and Willow were in the room with the girls. Bracken raced over

to Maia and started licking her face. Willow
charged to Sita's side and rubbed her head
against her. Holly, the spaniel, scurried under
the table fearfully.

Maia started to stroke the fox but then she
stopped. Why was she patting a fox? He seemed
very tame.

She looked around. Why was she in a cellar
with her friends? And why were there so many
animals? And why was that wildcat sitting
on poor Auntie Mabel's chest and hissing
furiously at her? "What's happening?" she said
in confusion.

"Maia!" the fox said, nuzzling her cheek. "Are you all right?"

Maia blinked. She could have sworn she'd just heard him say her name. But that couldn't be right. Animals couldn't talk. She stood up and backed away from the fox. "What … what's going on?" she said faintly. She realized she was holding a dark sparkling stone in her hand and dropped it.

The red squirrel raced over and grabbed it in his paws.

"Stay where you are, Auntie Mabel. I command you to freeze!" Sita said to Auntie Mabel as she lunged at the squirrel.

Auntie Mabel stopped with a jerk.

"What's happening?" Ionie said. "Why's Maia being weird?"

"I didn't silence Auntie Mabel in time," said Sita. "I think she said the spell – and now Maia's forgotten everything about magic."

"Magic?" Maia echoed in confusion. "What

are you talking about? Magic isn't real."

Seeing her friends exchange horrified looks, she buried her face in her hands. This was all too weird. Her head felt like it was spinning and she was filled with an intense sense of loss but she didn't know what for.

All four animals bounded over to her.

"Maia, it's a spell!"

Looking up, she saw that it was the fox speaking. He was staring at her intently with unusual indigo eyes.

"You can still get your memories back," said the wildcat. "Fight against the spell."

"You can do it, Maia," said the deer.

"We need you," said the squirrel, jumping on to her shoulder and stroking her hair with his little paws. "Please try."

All of the animals were talking now! How strange this was.

"What memories?" said Maia. "I don't understand."

The fox put his
paws up on her legs.
She stroked him. It was
strange – she felt as if she
knew him really well.

"Maia – magic is real," said
Lottie. "We're Star Friends."

"We've had lots of adventures
together," added Ionie. "We've fought
Shades and sent them back to the shadows.
Please believe us."

Maia looked into her green eyes. Ionie did
usually tell the truth, and fuzzy memories were
staring to flash into her head of she and her
friends doing magic. She frowned.

"Maia," Sita said. "The other day I promised
I'd never use magic on you but I'm going to
break my promise. You made me believe in
my magic powers earlier today and now I'm
going to make you do something – I'm going
to make you listen. Maia, you must believe us.

Magic *is* real."

More images formed in Maia's head. She and her friends in the clearing in the woods with the four animals… She and Ionie chasing after a gnome… Trying to catch little yellow stretchy men with fangs…

"Magic *is* real?" she said slowly.

Bracken licked her. "Yes. Please believe."

She looked into his sparkling eyes, framed by his soft rusty red fur, and felt the memories get stronger and more vivid. Crouching down, she hugged him and breathing in his sweet smell, her confusion cleared like a fog lifting. "Of course magic is real!" she said. "I'm your Star Friend – you're my Star Animal!"

"Always," said Bracken, nuzzling into her.

"All the things I'm remembering, they really happened, didn't they?" Maia said, looking at the others.

"Yes!" Lottie, Ionie and Sita said together.

"It depends rather on what you're imagining

but I presume so," said Sorrel dryly.

Maia felt a rush of love for all her friends and their animals. "Thank you for helping me," she said.

Bracken swung round and looked at Auntie Mabel, who was still frozen, unable to move, her eyes flashing furiously. "And that's why Star Friends are better than people who use dark magic," he said triumphantly to her. "Star Friends and their animals trust and help each other – and when they do they can defeat anything!"

Auntie Mabel glared at him, still under the power of Sita's command to be silent.

"Where's the Dark Stone?" Maia said.

"I've got it," said Juniper.

Maia walked back to Auntie Mabel. "Can you unfreeze her, Sita?"

"Are you sure?" Sita said.

"We've got to do something. We can't leave her frozen forever." Maia looked at Auntie

Mabel. "We'll give you a chance. If we unfreeze you, you have to do what we say and promise never to use dark magic again." She glanced at Sita. "Unfreeze her."

Sita pointed at Auntie Mabel. "You may move and speak."

"How dare you subdue me like that!" Auntie Mabel hissed at Sita.

"Do you promise that you will never use dark magic again?" Maia said.

"No!" said Auntie Mabel. Moving surprisingly quickly, she lunged for Juniper. He leaped away from her, keeping the stone safe.

"I command you to freeze!" cried Sita, pointing at her.

Auntie Mabel froze once more.

"Face me," said Sita calmly. "And open your hands."

Auntie Mabel did as she was told.

"Juniper, put the stone in Auntie Mabel's hands," Sita said.

"What?" Maia, Lottie and Ionie exclaimed.

"Sita, what are you doing?" Willow said.

"It's the only thing we *can* do if we want to keep Westcombe safe," said Sita softly. "Auntie Mabel, you will keep hold of the Dark Stone and say the spell to forget everything to do with magic."

Auntie Mabel tried to shake her head but couldn't. Only her eyes moved from side to side.

"Sita? Are you sure?" Lottie asked.

"It's using dark magic," said Juniper anxiously.

"It's making her use dark magic against herself," said Sita. She looked at them all steadily. "I really *am* sure this is the only way." Her voice rang with a new confidence. "We have to protect Westcombe."

"I agree with Sita," said Sorrel. The other animals nodded, too.

"Yes. Do it," Maia said.

"You may speak," said Sita to Auntie Mabel.

"Others will come," Auntie Mabel burst

out in a rush. "You can stop me but the village will not be safe. The clearing in the woods is a powerful magical place. You will face other threats more dangerous than me. You will—"

"Enough!" Sita commanded. "Say the spell that will make you forget! Say it now!"

Auntie Mabel's mouth moved and she looked like she was trying to keep it shut but the harsh words burst out of her in a tangled stream.

The stone glowed for a moment, and then Auntie Mabel's eyes clouded and she looked around in confusion.

"It worked!" breathed Lottie.

"That was incredible, Sita," said Maia in awe.

"What's happening?" Auntie Mabel said, looking dazed. "Why are we in my cellar?" She held out the Dark Stone. "And what's this?"

"That's mine," said Maia hurriedly, taking it from her. The stone felt icy cold and seemed to prickle her fingers. She shoved it in her pocket. She saw Holly still hiding under the table and had an idea. "We were here to help you with the decorations and then we heard a noise down here – it was the Patels' missing dog. I don't know how she got in here but we all came to get her and … then you banged your head."

Auntie Mabel blinked. "What about all these other animals?"

The Star Animals vanished.

Auntie Mabel blinked.

"What do you mean, Auntie Mabel?" Maia asked innocently.

Auntie Mabel rubbed her eyes. "I thought I saw wild animals… Goodness, I really did bang my head, didn't I?"

"You did. How about we go upstairs and we

can make you a cup of tea?" Lottie said.

"I think that would be a good idea," said Auntie Mabel faintly.

"And then we should take Holly home to the Patels," said Sita, crouching down and holding her hand out to the spaniel. "Come here, Holly. It's OK now. Come out."

Holly crept out and Sita picked her up. The spaniel licked her face, immediately calming down as Sita stroked and soothed her.

"The Winter Fayre!" said Auntie Mabel suddenly. "I need to take the decorations there."

"Don't worry, we'll sort that out for you," said Maia as they went upstairs. "You can have a rest and come to the fayre later, when you're feeling better."

Auntie Mabel smiled. "That's very kind of you, dears. Thank you very much."

CHAPTER FOURTEEN

"What are we going to do about the
decorations?" Maia whispered to the others
when Auntie Mabel was settled with a cup of
tea. "We can't let them be sold at the fayre."

"I have an idea," said Lottie. She turned
to Auntie Mabel and picked up one of the
decorations. "Um, I think there might be a
problem with these decorations."

"What sort of problem?" Auntie Mabel said.

"It's the crystals in the centre of the eyes. I
showed the decoration you gave me to my mum

and she said it's a choking hazard for children."

Auntie Mabel looked worried. "Oh dear, I hadn't thought of that. I put them on because … because…" She frowned. "Well, I think I must have thought they looked pretty. Yes, that must be why."

"We could always take them off for you," said Lottie. "The decorations will look just as cute without the sparkly crystals."

"It really would be best," Ionie added quickly as Auntie Mabel hesitated.

"Well, if you don't mind," said Auntie Mabel. "It's a shame – but I would hate a child to get hurt."

The four girls worked quickly. Soon all the crystals were sealed in a bag that Bracken buried deep in a flower bed in the garden and the decorations were nothing more than just normal Christmas decorations.

"We'll take them to the village hall," said Sita. "And we'll take Holly home on the way."

They created a makeshift lead for Holly using a piece of thick ribbon from Auntie Mabel's sewing box and then waved Auntie Mabel goodbye.

★ ★ ★

When they reached the Patels', the family were overjoyed to see Holly.

"Where did you find her?" Mrs Patel asked as her two little girls hugged the spaniel in delight and Holly bounded around them.

"In the woods," Maia said. They'd all decided that would be the best story.

"Thank you so much for bringing her back," said Mrs Patel.

"No problem!" the girls chorused.

The girls went on to the village hall and delivered the decorations. Maia's mum was already there. "I'm very glad you're here, girls," she said. "We could do with some extra help."

They were immediately swept up into getting the hall ready, the stalls put out and the coffee things set up in the kitchen. At two o'clock the hall doors were opened and people flocked in. Soon the whole place was full of people buying gifts, drinking tea and coffee, eating cakes and chatting. The smell of gingerbread and candyfloss filled the air.

Maia's mum came up to her with Alfie. He was wearing a Father Christmas hat and eating iced gingerbread. "The fayre's going so well," said Mrs Greene happily. "Granny Anne would be really pleased to know everything was carrying on just as she would have wanted."

"Mmm," Maia said, glancing over at where Auntie Mabel was selling her decorations. She had a feeling her granny would be even more pleased to know that they had managed to stop Auntie Mabel's evil plans!

We'll have to keep a close eye on her in case the spell wears off, Maia thought. *And we need to think about what to do with the Dark Stone.*

"Do you want to buy some gingerbread to have with your friends?" her mum said. "Ionie, Lottie and Sita are over there." She got some money out of her purse.

"Thanks, Mum! Is it OK if we go for a walk?" Maia said.

"Sure, I'll see you back at home later."

Maia ran to join the others and they bought slabs of warm gingerbread covered with sweet white icing then headed for the clearing, munching happily. No one said a thing about what had happened with Auntie Mabel. It was as though they all had a silent agreement not to speak about it until they reached the privacy of the clearing and could call their Star Animals.

They hurried down the track, past Granny Anne's cottage with a "For Sale" board up and along the overgrown footpath. Dark green ivy scrambled through the holly bushes, with their red berries providing splashes of colour against all the dull green and brown.

As they hurried into the clearing the girls called their animals' names and the four Star Animals appeared. Willow bucked joyfully, Juniper raced up a tree, Sorrel rolled on her back in a patch of winter sunlight and Bracken chased his bushy tail.

"We did it!" said Sita, breathing a sigh of relief.

"Yep," said Ionie. "Though we must remember to get rid of the decorations in our houses, too."

"And from my gran's," said Sita.

Maia nodded. "Once we've got rid of them – and decided what to do with the Dark Stone – everyone will be safe."

"Until some new threat comes along," said Lottie. "Do you think Auntie Mabel was right and more evil will come here?"

"If it does, we'll stop it!" Ionie declared.

"I'm sure you'll be able to, Ionie," Sorrel said, weaving between her legs. "You saved the day today by turning into that Shade. And it was you who realized you could smash the globe."

Maia waited for Lottie to roll her eyes as she usually did when Sorrel boasted about Ionie but she didn't. She smiled and linked arms with Ionie. "Sorrel's right – you were amazing, Ionie."

"It wasn't just me," said Ionie. "You were

brilliant when you snatched the Dark Stone and Maia was amazing when she fought off the magic spell…"

"Only thanks to all of you," Maia put in.

"You were awesome, too, Sita," Ionie went on. "If you hadn't commanded Auntie Mabel, I don't know what would have happened."

Sita blushed. "I wouldn't have been able to do it without Maia. She made me realize why the magic wasn't working. I just had to believe."

Maia glanced round and remembered something Auntie Mabel had said. "Is this clearing really powerful like Auntie Mabel told us, Bracken? Will it attract other people wanting to do dark magic?"

"It might," said Bracken. "It's a crossing place – a place where the Star World and the human world meet. It contains a lot of power…"

"And power will always attract people who want to use it for their own evil ends," said Sorrel seriously. "We must all be on our guard."

"But those people aren't here yet," said Juniper. "So for now, let's play!" He scampered away and Lottie raced after him, using her magic to climb a tree just as fast as him.

"Who wants a game of tag?" she called, hanging down from a branch.

"Me!" said Ionie to Maia's surprise. "Only if I can shadow-travel though," she added with a grin. "You're way too fast otherwise."

"OK," said Lottie. "Catch me if you can!" She swung through the branches before dropping down to the clearing floor. She landed in a patch of shadows and squealed as Ionie popped straight up and tagged her.

"Got you!" Ionie said, laughing.

Sita giggled. "One–nil to Ionie," she said, sitting down on a tree stump and putting her arm over Willow's back. "Willow and I will keep the score! We don't have a chance of keeping up with you." Willow snuggled against her happily.

Bracken nestled into Maia's arms and licked her face.

"I'm so glad I didn't lose you today," she told him, remembering how awful she had felt when she thought she might never see him again.

He wriggled deeper into her arms. "I hated being stuck in that snow globe and not being able to get to you. I never want that to happen again."

Maia hugged him tightly. "It won't. We'll keep each other safe."

"Forever," Bracken promised. "Whatever comes."

Maia's heart swelled joyfully. She loved being able to do magic with Lottie, Ionie and Sita, and being able to help and protect people, but most of all she loved having Bracken as her Star Animal.

"I love you," she whispered to him.

He squirmed in delight and licked her nose.

"Come on, Maia!" shouted Lottie. "Come and play!"

Maia grinned at Bracken. "Shall we join in?"

He nodded and jumped down from her arms. Bounding across the clearing, he leaped on top of Sorrel. "Time to play, pussycat!"

Sorrel yowled indignantly and sprang to her feet. Bracken tried to run off but Sorrel was too fast. They rolled across the ground play-fighting while Willow shook her head and Juniper scampered round them excitedly.

Fizzing with happiness, Maia ran to join her friends.